# GULLIVER'S TRAVELS

BY *Jonathan Swift*  ILLUSTRATED BY *David Small*

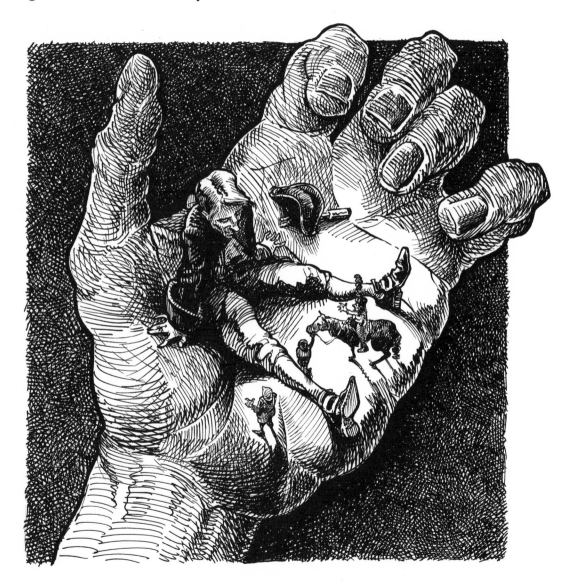

*William Morrow & Company / New York / 1983*

Printed in the United States of America.

1  2  3  4  5  6  7  8  9  10

Library of Congress Cataloging in Publication Data
Swift, Jonathan, 1667-1745. Gulliver's travels.
Summary: On two voyages, an Englishman becomes shipwrecked in a land where people are six inches high, and stranded in a land of giants. [1. Fantasy.   2. Size and shape—Fiction]   I. Small, David, 1945-    ill. II. Title.
PZ7.S979Gu   1983   [Fic]   83-1033
ISBN 0-688-02044-5
ISBN 0-688-02045-3 (lib. bdg.)

*To Sherry*

# PART ONE

## A Voyage to Lilliput

# CHAPTER ONE

My father had a small estate in Nottinghamshire. I was the third of five sons. He sent me to Emanuel College in Cambridge at fourteen, and after studying there three years, I was apprenticed to Mr. James Bates, a famous surgeon in London, with whom I continued four years. My father sent me small sums of money, and I spent them in learning navigation and other arts useful to those who intend to travel, as I always believed it would be my fortune to do.

When I left Mr. Bates, I was recommended by him to be ship's surgeon to the *Swallow*, on which I voyaged three years and a half. When I came back, I settled in London with the help of Mr. Bates and married Miss Mary Burton, second daughter to Mr. Edmond Burton, hosier.

But my good master Bates died two years after. I therefore consulted with my wife and determined to go again to sea. After several voyages to the East and West Indies, I accepted an offer from Captain William Prichard, master of the *Antelope*, who was making a voyage to the South Sea. We set sail from Bristol May 4, 1699, and in our passage to the East Indies, we were driven by a violent storm to the northwest of Van Diemen's Land.

On the fifth of November the seamen spied a rock within 120 yards of the ship, but the wind was so strong that we were driven directly upon it and immediately split.

Six of the crew, of whom I was one, let down

the boat into the sea to get clear of the ship and the rock. We rowed about ten miles, until we were able to work no longer. In about half an hour the boat was upset by a sudden storm from the north. What became of my companions, I cannot tell, but conclude they were all lost.

For my own part, I swam as fortune directed me and was pushed forward by wind and tide. I often let my legs drop and could feel no bottom. But when I was able to struggle no longer, I found myself within my depth, and by this time the storm was much abated.

I walked nearly a mile before I got to the shore, about eight o'clock in the

evening. I then advanced nearly half a mile inland, but could not discover any sign of houses or inhabitants. I was extremely tired, and with the heat of the weather, found myself much inclined to sleep. I lay down on the grass where I slept sounder than ever I remember having done in my life.

When I awoke, it was just daylight. I attempted to rise, but was not able to stir—for I found my arms and legs were strongly fastened on each side to the ground, and my hair, which was long and thick, tied down in the same manner. I heard a confused noise about me, but I could see nothing except the sky.

Soon I felt something alive moving on my left leg, advancing gently forward over my breast and coming almost up to my chin. Bending my eyes downwards as much as I could, I saw it to be a human creature not six inches high, with a bow and arrow in his hands and a quiver at his back. In the meantime, I felt at least forty more of the same kind following the first. I was in the utmost astonishment and roared so loud that they all ran back in a fright. Some of them were hurt with the falls they got by leaping from my sides upon the ground. However, they soon returned, and one of them, who ventured so far as to get a full sight of my face, cried out in a shrill but distinct voice, "Hekina degul."

At length, struggling to get loose, I succeeded in breaking the strings that fastened my left arm to the ground. At the same time, with a violent pull which gave me great pain, I loosened the strings that tied down my hair so that I was just able to turn my head about two inches. But the creatures ran off a second time, before I could seize them, whereupon there was a great

shout, and in an instant I felt more than a hundred arrows discharged on my left hand. They pricked me like so many needles. When this shower of arrows was over, I groaned with grief and pain, and then, when I strove again to get loose, they discharged another volley of arrows larger than the first, and some of them tried to stick me in the sides with spears.

By this time, I thought it most prudent to lie still until night, when, my left hand being already loose, I could easily free myself. But fortune disposed otherwise. When the people observed I was quiet, they discharged no more arrows. But by the increasing noise, I knew their numbers were greater, and I heard a knocking, like people at work, for over an hour.

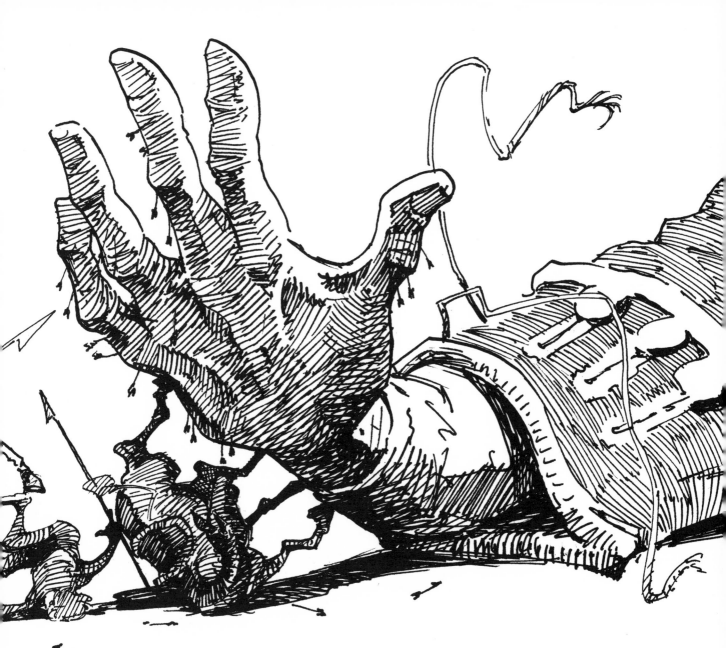

Turning my head that way as far as the pegs and strings would permit me, I saw a stage erected. From this, one of the inhabitants, who seemed to be a person of quality, made a long speech. I understood not one syllable.

He appeared to be of a middle age, and somewhat longer than my middle finger. He acted every bit an orator, and I could tell from his manner that he sometimes threatened me and sometimes spoke with pity and kindness. I answered in the most submissive manner, and, being almost famished with hunger, I could not help showing my impatience by putting my finger frequently on my mouth to signify that I wanted food.

He understood me well, and descending from the stage, commanded that several ladders should be set against my sides. More than a hundred of the inhabitants mounted the ladders and walked towards my mouth laden with baskets full of meat.

These had been sent by the king's orders when he first received word of me. I observed the flesh of several animals but could not distinguish them by taste. There were shoulders, legs, and loins shaped like those of mutton but smaller than the wings of a lark. I ate them two or three at a mouthful, and took three loaves at a time, about the bigness of musket-bullets. The inhabitants supplied me as fast as they could, showing astonishment at my appetite. I then made another sign that I wanted drink. They found by my eating that a small quantity would not satisfy me, and being most ingenious, they slung up one of their largest barrels of wine, then rolled it towards my hand, and beat out the top. I drank it off at a draught, for it hardly held half a pint.

After some time, there appeared before me a person of high rank sent by his Imperial Majesty. His excellency, having mounted my right leg, advanced to my face with about a dozen of his retinue and spoke about ten minutes, often pointing forwards, towards the capital city, about half a mile distant, where it had been decided by his Majesty that I must be transported.

Soon after, I heard a general shout, with frequent repetitions of the words, "Peplom selan," and felt great numbers of people on my left side relaxing the cords.

Then they daubed my face and both my hands with a sort of ointment very pleasant to the smell, which in a few minutes removed all the sting of their arrows. The relief from pain and hunger made me drowsy, and I presently fell asleep. I slept about eight hours, as I was told afterwards, and it was no wonder—for the physicians, by the emperor's order, had mingled a sleeping potion in the wine.

It seems that when I was first discovered sleeping on the ground after my landing, the emperor had early notice of it by a messenger, and he determined that I should be tied in the manner I have related, that plenty of meat and drink should be sent me and that a machine should be prepared to carry me to the capital city.

Five hundred carpenters and engineers were immediately set at work to

prepare the greatest engine they had. It was a frame of wood raised three inches from the ground, about seven feet long and four wide, moving upon twenty-two wheels. The difficulty was to place me on this vehicle.

Eighty poles, each one foot high, were erected for this purpose, and very strong cords were fastened by hooks to bandages, which the workmen had tied around my neck, hands, body and legs. Nine hundred of the strongest men were employed to draw up these cords by pulleys fastened on the poles, and thus in less than three hours, I was raised and slung into the en-

gine and there tied fast. Fifteen hundred of the emperor's largest horses, each about four and a half inches high, were then employed to draw me towards the capital city. All this was done while I lay in a deep sleep.

We rested at night with five hundred guards on each side of me. At sunrise we continued our march and arrived within two hundred yards of the city gates about noon. The emperor and all his court came out to meet us, but his officers would by no means allow his Majesty to risk his person by mounting upon my body.

Where the carriage stopped, there stood an ancient temple, the largest in the whole kingdom, and here it was determined I should lodge.

The great gate, through which I could easily creep, was about four feet high and almost two feet wide. On each side of the gate was a small window not more than six inches from the ground. Into one of these the king's blacksmiths fixed ninety-one chains, like those attached to a lady's watch in Europe, which were locked to my left leg with six and thirty padlocks.

More than a hundred thousand inhabitants came out of the town to have an opportunity of viewing me, and in spite of my guards, I believe there were at least ten thousand, at different times, who mounted upon my body by the help of ladders. But a proclamation was soon issued to forbid it, upon pain of death.

When the workmen found it was impossible for me to break loose, they cut all the strings that bound me. Then I rose up, feeling as melancholy as ever I had in my life. The noise and astonishment of the people at seeing me rise and walk are inexpressible. The chains that held my left leg were about two yards long, and gave me not only the freedom to walk backwards and forwards in a semi-circle, but allowed me to creep in and lie at full length inside the temple.

# CHAPTER TWO

When I came out of my house, the emperor was advancing on horseback towards me. He is taller, by almost the breadth of my nail, than any of his court, which alone is enough to strike awe into the beholders. His features are strong, his complexion olive, his body well proportioned, graceful, and majestic.

The better to behold him, I lay on my side, so that my face was parallel to his, and he stood but three yards off. His dress was very plain, but he wore a light helmet of gold adorned with jewels and a plume. He held his sword to defend himself if I should happen to break loose. It was almost three inches long, and the hilt and scabbard were gold enriched with diamonds. His voice was shrill but very clear. His Imperial Majesty spoke often to me, and I returned answers, but neither of us could understand a word.

After about two hours the court retired and I was left with a strong guard. When some of the rabble dared to shoot their arrows at me as I sat on the ground, the colonel ordered six of the ringleaders to be seized and delivered them bound into my hands. I put five of them into my coat pocket. As to the sixth, I made a face as if I would eat him alive. The poor man screamed terribly and the colonel and his officers were in much pain, especially when they saw me take out my penknife. But I soon set them at ease, for, cutting the strings he was bound with, I set him gently on the ground, and away he ran. I treated the rest in the same manner, and my kindness was later very much to my advantage at court.

Towards night I got with some difficulty into my house, where I lay on the ground for about a fortnight, till a bed was prepared for me out of six hundred beds of the common measure.

Six hundred servants were given me, and three hundred tailors made me a suit of clothes after the fashion of the country. Moreover, six of his Majesty's greatest scholars were employed to teach me their language.

In about three weeks I had made great progress in my study. During this time, the emperor often honored me with his visits, and we began to converse together. The first words I learned were to express my desire, which I every day repeated on my knees, that he give me my liberty. His answer was that this must be a work of time, and that first I must swear peace with him and his kingdom. Then he told me I must be searched by two of his officers, for probably I carried several weapons about me.

These gentlemen, having pen, ink, and paper about them, made a list of everything they saw, which I afterwards translated into English. It is as follows:

In the right coat pocket of the great Man-Mountain we found only one great piece of coarse cloth, large enough to be a carpet for your Majesty's chief room of State.

In the left pocket, we saw a huge silver chest with a cover of the same metal, which we were not able to lift. We desired it should be opened, and one of us stepping into it found himself up to the mid-leg in a sort of dust, some of which, flying into our faces, sent us both a-sneezing.

In his right waistcoat pocket, we found a bundle of white thin substances, folded one over another, about the bigness of three men, tied with a strong cable and marked with black figures, which we humbly conceive to be writings. In the left there was a sort of engine, from the back of which extended twenty long poles, with which, we conjecture, the Man-Mountain combs his head.

In the left pocket were two black pillars irregularly shaped. Within

each of these was enclosed an enormous plate of steel. These we obliged him to show us because we feared they might be dangerous engines. He took them out of their cases and told us that in his own country his practice was to shave his beard with one and to cut his meat with the other.

There were two pockets we could not enter: these he called his fobs. Out of the right fob hung a great silver chain with a wonderful kind of engine at the bottom. We directed him to draw out whatever was at the end of that chain, which appeared to be a globe, half silver and half of some transparent metal. On the transparent side we saw strange figures and thought we could touch them until we found our

fingers stopped by that shining substance. This engine made an incessant noise, like that of a water-mill, and we conjecture it is either some unknown animal or the god that he worships, but probably the latter, because he told us that he seldom did anything without consulting it.

From the left fob he took out a net almost large enough for a fisherman, but made to open and shut like a purse. Inside we found several round pieces of yellow metal, which if they be of gold must be of immense value.

Having thus, in obedience to your Majesty's commands, diligently searched all his pockets, we observed a girdle about his waist made of the hide of some enormous animal. From this, on the left side, hung a sword of the length of five men.

This is an exact inventory of what we found about the body of the Man-Mountain, who treated us with great civility. Signed and sealed,

Clefren Frelock, Marsi Frelock.

When this inventory was read to the emperor, he directed me to give up my sword, which I took out, scabbard and all. I likewise gave up my watch, which the emperor was very curious to see. He commanded two of his tallest guards to bear it on a pole upon their shoulders, as men in England do a barrel of ale.

I then gave up my purse with nine large pieces of gold, my knife and razor, my comb and silver snuffbox, my handkerchief and journal book. My sword was conveyed in carriages to his Majesty's warehouse. The rest of my goods were returned to me.

I had one private pocket which escaped their search. It contained a pair of spectacles and a pocket spyglass, which, being of no consequence to the emperor, I did not think myself bound in honor to reveal.

# CHAPTER THREE

My gentleness and good behavior had so pleased the emperor and his court, that I began to have hopes of getting my liberty. The natives too came by degrees to be less fearful of any danger from me. I would sometimes lie down and let five or six of them dance on my hand. And at last the boys and girls would venture to come and play hide and seek in my hair.

One day, the emperor entertained me with several of the country's shows. I was most diverted by the rope-dance, performed upon a slender white thread two feet long and twelve inches from the ground.

This diversion is only practised by those persons who are candidates for great employments and high favor at court. When a great office is vacant, five or six of those candidates ask the emperor if they may entertain his Majesty and the court with a dance on the rope, and whoever jumps the highest without falling, succeeds in the office. Very often the chief ministers themselves are commanded to show their skill and to convince the emperor that they have not lost their faculty.

There is likewise another diversion, which is only shown before the emperor and empress and first minister upon particular occasions. The emperor lays on a table three fine silken threads six inches long. One is blue, the other red and the third green. These threads are proposed as prizes for those persons whom the emperor has a mind to distinguish by a peculiar mark of his favor.

The ceremony is performed in his Majesty's great chamber of State. The emperor holds a stick in his hands, parallel to the horizon, while the candidates sometimes leap over the stick, sometimes creep under it backwards and forwards several times, according to whether the stick is raised or lowered. Whoever performs his part with the most agility and holds out the longest in leaping and creeping, is rewarded with the blue-colored silk. The red is given to the next, and the green to the third.

I amused the emperor one day in a very extraordinary manner. I took nine sticks and fixed them firmly in the ground in a square. I took four other sticks and tied them parallel at each corner, about two feet from the ground. Then I fastened my handkerchief to the nine sticks that stood erect and extended it on all sides until it was as tight as the top of a drum.

I then desired the emperor to let a troop of his best horse, twenty-four in number, come and exercise upon this plain. His Majesty approved of the proposal and I took them up one by one, with the proper officers to exercise them. As soon as they got into order, they divided into two parties, performed mock skirmishes, discharged blunt arrows, drew their swords, fled and pursued, attacked and retired, and in short displayed the best military discipline I ever beheld.

The emperor was much delighted, and he persuaded the empress herself to let me hold her in her chair within two yards of the stage, from which she was able to view the whole performance.

Fortunately no accident happened in these entertainments—only once a fiery horse, pawing with his hoof, struck a hole in my handkerchief, and overthrew his rider and himself. The horse that fell was strained in the left shoulder, but the rider was not hurt, and I repaired my handkerchief as well as I could.

I had sent so many petitions for my liberty, that his Majesty mentioned the matter at length in a full council, where it was opposed by none except Skyresh Bolgolam, Admiral of the Realm, who was pleased, without any provocation, to be my mortal enemy. But it was carried against him by the whole board, and confirmed by the emperor. Skyresh then obtained that the conditions on which I should be set free should be drawn up by himself.

After they were read, I was required to swear to them in the manner prescribed by their laws. This was to hold my right foot in my left hand, to place the middle finger of my right hand on the crown of my head, and my thumb on the tip of my right ear. Because the reader may be curious, I have made a translation of these conditions:

*Most mighty emperor of Lilliput, delight and terror of the universe, whose dominions extend to the extremities of the globe; monarch of all monarchs; taller than the sons of men; whose feet press down to the center, and whose head*

strikes against the sun; at whose nod the princes of the earth shake their knees; pleasant as the spring, comfortable as the summer, fruitful as autumn, dreadful as winter. His most sublime Majesty proposeth to the Man-Mountain, lately arrived at our celestial dominions, the following articles, which by a solemn oath he shall be obliged to perform.

### I

The Man-Mountain shall not depart from our dominions, without our license under the great seal.

### II

He shall not presume to come into our metropolis, without our express order, at which time, the inhabitants shall have two hours warning to keep within their doors.

### III

The said Man-Mountain shall confine his walks to our principal high roads, and not walk or lie down in a meadow, or field of corn.

### IV

As he walks the roads, he shall take the utmost care not to trample upon the bodies of any of our loving subjects, their horses, or carriages, nor take any of our subjects into his hands, without their consent.

### V

If a message require extraordinary speed, the Man-Mountain shall be obliged to carry in his pocket the messenger and horse, a six days' journey once in every moon, and return the said messenger back (if so required) safe.

### VI

He shall be our ally against our enemies in the island of Blefuscu, and do his utmost to destroy their fleet, which is now preparing to invade us.

## LASTLY

*That upon his solemn oath to observe all the above articles, the Man-Mountain shall have a daily allowance of meat and drink, sufficient for the support of 1724 of our subjects, and free access to our royal person, and other marks of our favor.*

*Given at our palace at Belfaborac the twelfth day of the ninety-first moon of our reign.*

I swore and subscribed to these articles with great cheerfulness, whereupon my chains were immediately unlocked, and I was at full liberty.

# CHAPTER FOUR

One morning, about two weeks after I had obtained my liberty, Reldresal, secretary of private affairs, came to my house, attended by only one servant. He ordered his coach to wait and asked if I would give him an hour's audience. I offered to lie down, that he might the more conveniently reach my ear, but he chose rather to let me hold him in my hand during our conversation. He began with compliments on my liberty, but he added that if it had not been for the present situation of things at court, perhaps I might not have obtained it so soon. "For," said he, "flourishing as our condition may appear to foreigners, we are in danger of an invasion from the island of Blefuscu, which is the other great empire of the universe, almost as large and powerful as this of his Majesty.

"Our histories of six thousand moons make no mention of any regions other than the two great empires of Lilliput and Blefuscu, which have been engaged in a most obstinate war. It began in the following way.

"It is agreed by everyone that the primitive way of breaking eggs before we eat them is upon the larger end—but his present Majesty's grandfather, while he was a boy, going to eat an egg and breaking it according to the ancient practice, happened to cut one of his fingers. Whereupon the emperor, his father, made a law commanding his subjects to break the smaller end of their eggs.

"The people so highly resented this law that, there have been six rebellions raised on that account, wherein one emperor lost his life and another his crown. It is calculated that eleven thousand persons have suffered death rather than break their eggs at the smaller end.

"The Big-Endians have found so much encouragement at the Emperor of Blefuscu's court, that a bloody war has been carried on between the two empires for six and thirty moons. They have now equipped a large fleet, and are preparing to descend upon us. Therefore, his Imperial Majesty, placing great confidence in your valor and strength, has commanded me to lay this before you."

I asked the secretary to let the emperor know that I was ready, at the risk of my life, to defend him against all invaders.

# CHAPTER FIVE

I communicated to his Majesty a project of seizing the enemy's whole fleet which, our scouts assured us, lay at anchor in the harbor ready to sail with the first fair wind.

The empire of Blefuscu, is an island to the north-northeast of Lilliput, separated only by a channel eight hundred yards wide. I consulted the most experienced seamen on the depth of the channel, and they told me that in the middle at high water it was seventy *glumgluffs* deep, which is about six feet of European measure.

I walked to the coast, where, lying down behind a hillock, I took out my spyglass and viewed the enemy's fleet at anchor—about fifty men-of-war and a great number of other vessels.

I then came back to my house and gave order for a great quantity of the strongest cable and bars of iron. The cable was about as thick as packthread, and the bars were the length and size of a knitting-needle. I tripled the cable to make it stronger, and for the same reason I twisted three of the iron bars together, bending the ends into a hook. Having thus fixed fifty hooks to as many cables, I went back to the coast and taking off my coat, shoes, and stockings, walked into the sea. I waded with what haste I could, swimming in the middle about thirty yards until I felt the ground, arriving near the fleet in less than half an hour.

The enemy were so frightened when they saw me, that they leaped out of their ships and swam to shore. Then, fastening a hook to the hole at the prow of each ship, I tied all the cords together at the end. Meanwhile, the enemy discharged several thousand arrows, many of which stuck in my hands and face.

My greatest fear was for my eyes, which I should have lost if I had not suddenly thought of the pair of spectacles which had escaped the emperor's searchers. These I took out and fastened upon my nose. Thus armed I went on boldly with my work in spite of the enemy's arrows, many of which struck against the glasses of my spectacles.

Then, taking the knot in my hand, I began to pull. But not a ship would stir, for they were held fast by their anchors. Thus the boldest part of my

enterprise remained. Letting go the cord, I resolutely cut with my knife the cables that fastened the anchors, receiving about two hundred arrows in my face and hands. Then I again took up the knotted end of the cables to which my hooks were tied and with great ease drew fifty of the enemy's largest men of war after me.

When the Blefuscudians saw the whole fleet moving and me pulling at the end, they set up a scream of despair that is almost impossible to describe.

When I had got out of danger, I stopped to pick out the arrows that stuck in my hands and face and rubbed on some of the ointment that was given me at my first arrival. I then took off my spectacles, and after waiting about an hour until the tide was fallen, I waded through the middle with my cargo and arrived safe at the royal port of Lilliput.

The emperor and his whole court stood on the shore awaiting me. They saw the ships move forward but they could not discern me, as I was in the middle of the channel with water up to my neck. The emperor concluded that I was drowned and that the enemy's fleet was approaching in a hostile manner. But he was soon set at ease, for, the channel growing shallower every step I made, I came in a short time within hearing, and holding up the end of the cable by which the fleet was fastened, I cried in a loud voice, "Long live the Emperor of Lilliput!"

The prince received me at my landing with all possible joy and made me a Nardac upon the spot, which is the highest title of honor among them.

His Majesty then asked me to take some other opportunity of bringing all the rest of his enemy's ships into his ports. He seemed to think of nothing less than becoming the sole monarch of the whole world.

I plainly protested that I would never be the means of bringing a free and brave people into slavery. And though the wisest ministers were of my opinion, my open refusal was so opposite to his Imperial Majesty that he could never forgive me. And from this time began a plot between his Majesty, and those of his ministers who were my enemies, which nearly ended in my utter destruction.

About three weeks after this exploit, there arrived an embassy from Blefuscu with humble offers of a peace. This was soon concluded upon conditions very advantageous to our emperor. There were six ambassadors, with a train of about five hundred persons, all very magnificent.

Having been privately told how much I had befriended them, they made me a visit, paying me many compliments and inviting me to that kingdom in their emperor's name. Accordingly, the next time I had the honor to see our emperor, I asked his permission to visit the Blefuscudian monarch. This was granted me, but in a very cold manner, of which I afterward learned the reason.

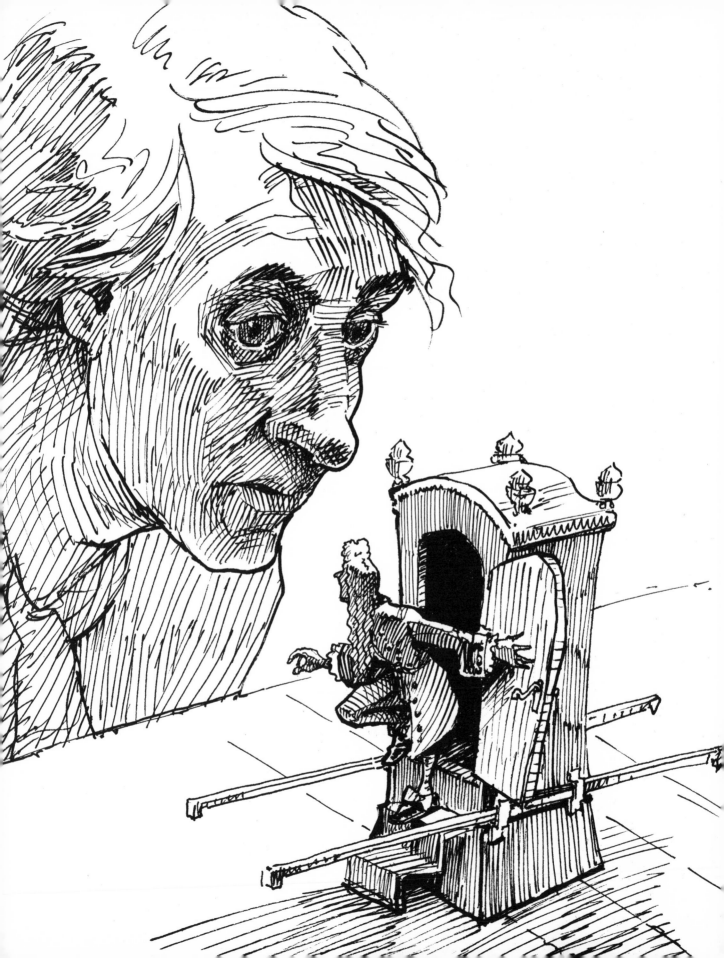

# CHAPTER SIX

When I was just preparing to pay my attendance on the Emperor of Blefuscu, a distinguished person at court (to whom I had once done a great service) came to my house very privately at night in a sedan chair.

I put the chair, with his lordship in it, into my coat pocket, and giving orders to a servant to admit no one, I fastened the door, placed my visitor on the table and sat down by it. His lordship's face was full of concern.

I enquired into the reason and he asked me to hear him with patience in a matter that highly concerned my honor and my life.

"You are aware," he said, "that Skyris Bolgolam has been your mortal enemy ever since your arrival. His hatred is much increased since your great success against Blefuscu, by which his glory, as admiral, is obscured. This lord and others have accused you of treason.

"Out of gratitude for the favors you have done me, I have brought a copy of the charges against you."

*Articles of impeachment against the Man-Mountain.*

### ARTICLE I

*Having brought the imperial fleet of Blefuscu into the royal port, he refused a command by his Imperial Majesty to seize all the other ships, and to put to death all the Big-Endian exiles, and also all the people of that empire who would not immediately agree to break their eggs at the smaller end.*

### ARTICLE II

*When ambassadors arrived from the court of Blefuscu, like a false traitor, he aided them, although he knew them to be servants to a prince lately in open war against his Majesty.*

### ARTICLE III

*Contrary to the duty of a faithful subject, he is now preparing to make a voyage to the court of Blefuscu, where he intends to aid the Emperor of Blefuscu, so recently an enemy.*

"In the several debates on this impeachment," my friend continued, "his Majesty often pointed out the services you had done him, while the treasurer and admiral insisted that you should be put to death. For a long time there was a majority against you, but his Majesty decided, if possible, to spare your life.

"Here, Reldresal, the secretary for private affairs, who had always shown himself your friend, suggested that if his Majesty would give orders to put out both your eyes, justice might be satisfied and all the world would applaud the lenience of the emperor.

"At this, Bolgolam, the admiral, rose up in fury, saying he wondered how the secretary could dare to preserve the life of a traitor. And the treasurer, pointing out the expense of maintaining you, also urged your death. But his Imperial Majesty was graciously pleased to say that since the council thought the loss of your eyes too easy, some other punishment might be inflicted. And your friend the secretary, in answer to what the treasurer had said concerning the great expense his Majesty had in maintaining you, suggested that his Excellency might gradually lessen your allowance so that for want of sufficient food you would grow weak and faint, lose your appetite and consequently die within a few months. Immediately upon your death, five or six thousand of his Majesty's subjects might, in two or three days, bury your flesh in different parts to prevent infection, leaving the skeleton as a monument to posterity.

"Thus, the whole affair was arranged. It was commanded that the plan of starving you by degrees should be kept a secret, but the sentence of putting out your eyes was entered on the books.

"In three days your friend the secretary will come to your house and read the articles of impeachment. Then he will point out the great lenience of his Majesty that only condemns you to the loss of your eyes. Twenty of his Majesty's surgeons will attend, in order to see the operation well performed, by discharging very sharp pointed arrows into your eyes as you lie on the ground.

"I leave to your judgement what measures you will take, and to avoid suspicion, I must immediately return in as private a manner as I came."

His lordship did so, and I remained alone, in great confusion. At first I was strongly bent upon resistance. For while I had liberty, I might easily with stones pelt the capital city to pieces, but I soon rejected that idea with horror, remembering the oath I had made to the emperor. Finally, having his Majesty's consent to pay my respects to the Emperor of Blefuscu, I went to that side of the island and between wading and swimming, arrived at the royal port of Blefuscu, where the people had long expected me.

His Majesty, attended by the royal family and officers of the court, came out to receive me. I lay on the ground to kiss his Majesty's and the empress's hand and told his Majesty that I had come according to my promise, to have the honor of seeing so mighty a monarch.

# CHAPTER SEVEN

Three days after my arrival, walking out of curiosity along the northeast coast of the island, I observed in the sea something that looked like a boat overturned. I pulled off my shoes and stockings, and wading two or three hundred yards, I plainly saw it to be a boat, which I supposed might by some storm have been driven from a ship.

After a huge amount of labor I managed to get my boat to the royal port of Blefuscu, where a great crowd of people appeared, full of wonder at the sight of so large a vessel. I told the emperor that good fortune had thrown this boat in my way to carry me to some place where I might return into my native country, and begged his Majesty's orders for materials to fix it up, which, after some kindly speeches, he was pleased to grant.

Five hundred workmen were employed to make two sails to my boat by quilting thirteen fold of their strongest linen together. I set myself to make ropes and cables by twisting ten, twenty or thirty of the strongest of theirs. A great stone that I happened to find after a search by the seashore served me for an anchor.

In about a month, I was ready to take my leave. The emperor and royal family came out of the palace. I lay down on my face to kiss his hand, which he very graciously gave me. His Majesty presented me with fifty purses of gold coins together with his picture which I put immediately into one of my gloves to keep it from being hurt.

I took with me six cows and two bulls, with as many ewes and rams, intending to carry them to my own country. And to feed them on board, I had a good bundle of hay and a bag of corn. I would gladly have taken a dozen of the natives, but this was a thing the emperor would not permit.

Having prepared all things as well as I was able, I set sail. When I had gone about twenty-four leagues from Blefuscu I saw a sail steering to the southeast. I hailed her but could get no answer. Yet I found I gained upon her, for the wind eased, and in half an hour she saw me and discharged a gun. The ship slackened her sails and I came up with her between five and six in the evening, September 26, 1701, and my heart leapt within me to see her English colors.

I put my cows and sheep into my coat pockets and got on board with all my little cargo. The captain, Mr. John Biddel of Deptford, treated me with kindness and asked me to let him know what place I came from last. This I did in few words, but he thought I was raving mad. I took my black cattle and sheep out of my pocket, however, which after great astonishment clearly convinced him.

We arrived in England on the 13th of April, 1702. I stayed two months with my wife and family, but my insatiable desire to see foreign countries would allow me to remain no longer. I left fifteen hundred pounds with my wife, and fixed her in a good house. Then, taking leave of my wife and boy and girl, with tears on both sides, I sailed on board the *Adventure*. But my account of this voyage must be found in the second part of my travels.

# PART TWO

## *A Voyage to Brobdingnag*

# CHAPTER ONE

Having been condemned by nature and fortune to an active and restless life, I again left my native country and took shipping in the Downs on the 20th day of June, 1702, in the *Adventure,* Capt. John Nicholas, commander, bound for Surat.

We had a good voyage until we passed the Straits of Madagascar, where the winds began to blow a constant gale which continued for twenty days. Then the wind ceased, and it was a perfect calm. But our captain, a man well experienced in the navigation of those seas, told us to prepare for a storm, which happened the day following when a southern wind, called a monsoon, began to set in.

During this storm, we were carried about five hundred leagues to the east. Even the oldest sailor on board could not tell in what part of the world we were. Our provisions held out well, our ship was sound and our crew in good health, but we lay in the utmost need for water.

On the 16th day of June, 1703, a boy on the topmast discovered land. On the 17th we came in full view of a great island or continent with a small neck of land jutting out into the sea and with a creek too shallow to hold a ship of above one hundred tons. We dropped anchor within a few miles of this creek, and our captain sent a dozen of his men in the long-boat with vessels for water. I asked to go with them, so that I might see the country and make what discoveries I could.

Our men wandered on the shore to look for some fresh water near the sea, and I walked alone about a mile on the other side, where I observed the country all barren and rocky. Seeing nothing to interest me, I returned toward the creek, where I saw our men, already in the boat and rowing for life to the ship.

I was going to call after them, when I observed a huge creature pursuing them as fast as he could. He took enormous strides, but our men had a head start and the sea being full of sharp pointed rocks, the monster was not able to overtake the boat.

I ran as fast as I could and climbed up a steep hill which gave me a view of the country. I found it fully cultivated, but what took me by surprise was the length of the grass, which was above twenty feet high.

I found myself on what I took to be a highway, although it served to the inhabitants only as a footpath through a field of barley. I was an hour walking to the end of this field, which was fenced in with a hedge at least 120 feet high.

There were steps to climb from this field into the next, yet it was impossible for me to climb them because every step was six feet high and the upper one was more than twenty.

I was trying to find some gap in the hedge, when I noticed one of the inhabitants in the next field. He appeared as tall as an ordinary church steeple, and he took about ten yards at every stride, as near as I could guess. I was struck with the utmost fear and astonishment, and ran to hide myself in the corn, where I saw him at the top of the steps, looking back into the next field. I heard him call in a voice louder than a speaking trumpet, but the noise was so high in the air that at first I thought it was thunder.

Then seven monsters like himself came toward him with reaping-hooks in their hands, each hook about the size of six scythes. These people were not so well clad as the first, whose laborers they seemed to be. And at some words he spoke, they went to reap the corn in the field where I lay.

I kept from them at as great a distance as I could, but was forced to move with extreme difficulty, for I could hardly squeeze my body between the stalks of the corn. I heard the reapers not more than a hundred yards behind me.

Being overcome by despair, I lay down between two ridges, and wished I might there end my days. In this terrible state of mind I could not help thinking of Lilliput, whose inhabitants looked upon me as the greatest being that ever appeared in the world, and where I had been able to draw an imperial fleet in my hand.

One of the reapers approached within ten yards of the ridge where I lay, and with his next step I knew I would be squashed to death or cut in two with his reaping-hook. And therefore when he was again about to move, I screamed as loud as fear could make me.

The huge creature looked round about him for some time and at last spied me. He considered me awhile with the caution of one who tries to catch hold of a small dangerous animal in such a manner that it shall not be

able either to scratch or bite him, as I myself have sometimes done with a weasel in England. At length he picked me up and brought me within three yards of his eyes, that he might better behold my shape.

I guessed his meaning, and this gave me so much presence of mind that I resolved not to struggle in the least, as he held me in the air above sixty feet from the ground, although he painfully pinched my sides for fear I should slip through his fingers. All I ventured was to raise my eyes toward the sun and place my hands together as if I were praying and speak some words in a humble tone suitable to the condition I then was in. Immediately he ran along with me to his master, who was a substantial farmer, and the same person I had first seen in the field.

The farmer called his hands about him and asked them (I afterwards learned) whether they had ever seen any little creature that resembled me. He then placed me softly on the ground upon all fours. But I immediately got up and walked slowly backwards and forwards, to let those people see I had no intention of running away.

They all sat down in a circle about me, the better to observe my motions. I pulled off my hat and made a low bow toward the farmer. I fell on my knees and lifted up my hands and eyes and spoke several words as loud as I could.

By this time the farmer was convinced I must be a rational creature. He spoke often to me, but the sound of his voice pierced my ears like that of a water-mill, yet his words were articulate enough. I answered as loudly as I could in several languages, and he often laid his ear within two yards of me, but all in vain, for we could not understand each other. He then sent his servants to their work, and taking his handkerchief out of his pocket, he spread it on his hand, which he placed on the ground palm upward, making me a sign to step on it. I thought it my part to obey, and for fear of falling, I laid myself full length upon the handkerchief. In this manner he carried me home.

There he called his wife, and showed me to her—but she screamed and ran back, as women in England do at the sight of a spider. However, when she had seen my behavior awhile, she grew extremely fond of me.

It was about noon, and a servant brought in dinner in a dish about four-and-twenty feet in diameter. The company were the farmer and wife, three children, and an old grandmother. When they had sat down, the farmer placed me at some distance from him on the table, which was thirty feet above the floor. I was in a terrible fright and kept as far as I could from the edge for fear of falling.

The wife minced a bit of meat, then crumbled some bread on a wooden platter and placed it before me. I made her a low bow, took out my knife and fork and fell to eating, which gave them great delight. The mistress sent her maid for a small cup, which held about two gallons, and filled it with drink. I took up the vessel with much difficulty in both hands and in a most respectful manner drank to her ladyship's health. Then, as I advanced to-

wards my master (as I shall call him), his youngest son, who sat next to him, a boy of about ten years old, took me up by the legs and held me so high in the air that I trembled in every limb. His father snatched me from him and at the same time gave him such a box on the left ear as would have felled a European troop of horse to the earth. He ordered him to be taken from the table. But, being afraid the boy might owe me a grudge, and well remembering how mischievous all children among us naturally are to sparrows, rabbits, young kittens and puppy-dogs, I fell on my knees, and pointing to the boy, made my master understand as well as I could that I desired his son be pardoned. The father complied, and the lad took his seat again, whereupon I went to him and kissed his hand, which my master took, and made him stroke me gently with it.

In the midst of dinner my mistress's favorite cat leapt into her lap. I heard a noise behind me like that of a dozen stocking-weavers at work, and turning my head I found it proceeded from the purring of this animal who seemed to be three times larger than an ox.

The fierceness of this creature's face frightened me. Although I stood at the further end of the table, more than fifty feet off, my mistress held her fast for fear she might give a spring and seize me in her talons. But as it happened there was no danger, for the cat took not the least notice of me when my master placed me close to her.

When dinner was almost done, the nurse came in with a child a year old in her arms who immediately saw me and began a squall that you might have heard from London Bridge to Chelsea to get me for a plaything. The mother took me up and put me towards the child, who seized me by the middle and got my head in his mouth, where I roared so loudly that the baby was frightened and let me drop. I should have surely broken my neck if the mother had not held her apron under me.

When dinner was done, my master went out to his laborers, and, as I could learn from his voice and gesture, gave his wife strict instructions to take care of me. I was very much tired, which my mistress saw. She put me on her own bed and covered me with a clean white handkerchief. It was larger and coarser than the mainsail of a man-of-war.

I had slept about two hours, and dreamed I was at home with my wife and children, which increased my sorrows, when I awoke and found myself alone in a vast room, between two and three hundred feet wide and above two hundred high. I was lying in a bed twenty yards wide. The bed was eight yards from the floor.

While I was under these circumstances, two rats crept up the curtains and ran backwards and forwards on the bed. One of them came up almost to my face, whereupon I drew out my sword to defend myself. These horrible animals had the boldness to attack me on both sides, and one of them had his forefeet at my collar, but I had the good fortune to rip up his belly before he could do me any mischief. The other, seeing the fate of his comrade, made his escape.

After this exploit, I walked gently to and fro on the bed to recover my breath and loss of spirits. Soon after, my mistress came into the room, and seeing me all bloody, she took me up in her hand. I pointed to the dead rat, smiling and making other signs to show I was not hurt. At this she was extremely happy and called the maid to take up the dead rat with a pair of tongs and throw it out of the window.

# CHAPTER TWO

My mistress had a daughter nine years old. Her mother and she prepared the baby's cradle for me for the night. The cradle was put into a small drawer of a cabinet and the drawer placed upon a hanging shelf for fear of the rats.

This young girl made me seven shirts of as fine cloth as could be got, which indeed was coarser than sackcloth, and these she constantly washed for me with her own hands. She was likewise my schoolmistress in teaching me the language. When I pointed to anything, she told me the name of it in her own tongue, so that, in a few days, I was able to call for whatever I had a mind to.

She was very good-natured, and not over forty feet high, being little for her age. She gave me the name of Grildrig, which the family took up, and afterwards the whole kingdom. The word means, in English, doll. To her I chiefly owe my preservation. We never parted while I was there. I called her my Glumdalclitch, or Little Nurse. And I should be guilty of great ingratitude if I omitted this mention of her care and affection towards me.

It now began to be known and talked of in the neighborhood that my master had found a strange animal in the field exactly shaped in every part like a human creature, which it likewise imitated in all its actions.

Another farmer who lived nearby came on a visit to enquire into the truth of this story. I was immediately produced and placed upon a table, where I walked as I was commanded, drew my sword, put it back again, made my greeting, asked him in his own language how he did, and told him he was welcome, just as my little nurse had instructed me. This man, who was old and dim-sighted, had the character of a great miser, and to my misfortune he gave my master the cursed advice to show me as a sight on market-day in the next town.

I guessed there was some mischief when I observed my master and his friend whispering and sometimes pointing at me. But the next morning Glumdalclitch told me about the whole matter, which she had cunningly found out from her mother. The poor girl laid me on her bosom and began

weeping with shame and grief. She feared some mischief would happen to me from rude folks who might squeeze me to death or break one of my limbs by taking me in their hands. She also knew what an indignity I should suffer to be exposed for money as a public spectacle.

My master, following the advice of his friend, carried me in a box the next market-day to the neighboring town. He took with him his little daughter, my nurse. The girl had been so thoughtful as to put the quilt of her doll's bed into the box for me to lie down on. However, I was terribly shaken in this journey, although it lasted only half an hour, for the horse went about forty feet at every step and trotted so high that the agitation was equal to the rising and falling of a ship in a great storm.

My master stopped at an inn which he used to frequent. There he hired the crier to give notice through the town of a strange creature, in every part of the body resembling a human creature, to be seen at the sign of the Green Eagle.

I was placed upon a table in the largest room of the inn, which might have been nearly three hundred feet square. My little nurse stood close to the table to take care of me and direct what I should do.

I walked about on the table as the girl commanded. She asked me questions, and I answered them as loudly as I could. I took up a thimble filled with liquor, which Glumdalclitch had given me for a cup, and drank to their health. I drew out my sword, and flourished with it after the manner of fencers in England.

I was that day shown to twelve sets of company, until I was half dead with weariness. For those who had seen me made such wonderful reports that the people were ready to break down the doors to come in. My master for his own interest would not allow anyone to touch me, except my nurse, and to prevent danger, benches were set round the table at such a distance as put me out of everybody's reach. However, a schoolboy aimed a hazelnut directly at my head, which very narrowly missed me. Otherwise it would have surely knocked out my brains, for it was almost as large as a pumpkin.

My master gave public notice that he would show me again the next market-day. In the meantime, he prepared a more convenient vehicle for me, for I was so tired with my first journey and with entertaining company that I could hardly stand or speak a word.

My master, finding how profitable I was likely to be, decided to show me to the largest cities of the kingdom. Having provided himself with all things necessary for a long journey, he took leave of his wife, and we set out for the capital city, which was about three thousand miles distance from our house.

My master made his daughter Glumdalclitch carry me on her lap in a box tied about her waist. The girl had lined it on all sides with the softest cloth she could get. She had furnished it with her doll's bed and provided me with linen and other necessities.

We made easy journeys of not above 150 miles a day, for Glumdalclitch, to spare me, complained she was tired from the trotting of the horse. She often took me out of my box to give me air and show me the country. We passed over five or six rivers many times broader and deeper than the Nile or the Ganges, and there was hardly a rivulet so small as the Thames at London Bridge. We were ten weeks in our journey, and I was shown in eighteen large towns, besides many villages and private families.

On the 26th day of October, we arrived at the metropolis, called in their language "Lorbrulgrud," or "Pride of the Universe." My master took a

lodging not far from the royal palace, and put out notices containing an exact description of my person and parts. He hired a large room and provided a table upon which I was to act my part. I was shown ten times a day, to the wonder and satisfaction of all. I could now speak the language tolerably well, and I perfectly understood every word that was spoken to me. Besides, I had learned their alphabet, for Glumdalclitch had been my instructor at leisure hours during our journey.

# CHAPTER THREE

The frequent labors I underwent every day made a very considerable change in my health—I was almost reduced to a skeleton. The farmer observed it, and concluding I soon must die, resolved to make as good a profit out of me as he could. While he was thus reasoning with himself, a gentleman came from court, commanding my master to bring me immediately for the diversion of the queen.

Her Majesty and those who attended her were delighted with my demeanor. I fell on my knees and begged the honor of kissing her imperial foot. Instead she held out her little finger toward me, which I embraced in both my arms and put the tip of it to my lips. She asked me questions about my country and travels, which I answered as distinctly as I could. She asked whether I would be content to live at court. I bowed down to the table and humbly answered that I was my master's slave, but if I were at my own disposal I should be proud to devote my life to her Majesty's service. She then asked my master whether he were willing to sell me. He, who thought I could not live a month, was ready enough to part with me and demanded a thousand pieces of gold, which were ordered for him on the spot.

I then said to the queen that since I was now her Majesty's most humble creature, I must beg as a favor that Glumdalclitch, who had always tended me with so much kindness, and understood how to do it so well, might be admitted into her service and continue to be my nurse and instructor. Her Majesty agreed to my petition and easily got the farmer's consent. He was glad enough to have his daughter employed at court, and the poor girl herself was not able to hide her joy. My late master withdrew, bidding me farewell, and saying he had left me in a good service. To this I answered not a word, only making him a slight bow.

The queen observed my coldness and asked me the reason. I made bold to tell her Majesty that I owed no other obligation to my late master than his not dashing out the brains of a harmless creature found by chance in his field and this obligation was amply repaid by the gain he had made in showing me through half the kingdom and the price he had now sold me for.

The queen took me in her own hand and carried me to the king. His Majesty ordered that particular care should be taken of me and was of opinion that Glumdalclitch should continue to tend me because, he observed, we had a great affection for each other. An apartment was provided for her at court. She had a governess for her education, a maid to dress her, and two other servants for menial duties. But the care of me was wholly given over to herself.

The queen commanded her own cabinet-maker to make a box that might serve me for a bed-chamber. This man was a most ingenious artist and in three weeks finished a wooden chamber of sixteen feet square and twelve high, with sash windows, a door, and two closets, like a London bed-chamber.

A precise workman, who was famous for little curiosities, undertook to make me two chairs of a substance not unlike ivory, and two tables, with a cabinet to put my things in. The room was quilted on all sides, as well as the floor and the ceiling, to prevent any accident from the carelessness of those who carried me.

The queen likewise ordered the thinnest silks that could be found, to make me clothes. They were not much thicker than an English blanket, and very cumbersome until I was accustomed to them.

The queen became so fond of my company that she could not dine without me. I had a table placed upon the same one at which her Majesty ate, just at her left elbow, and I had a chair to sit on. Glumdalclitch stood upon a stool on the floor near my table to assist me. I had a set of silver dishes and plates and other necessities, which, in proportion to those of the queen, were not much bigger than what I have seen in a London toyshop. These my little nurse kept in her pocket in a silver box and gave me at meals, always cleaning them herself.

Nothing angered and frightened me so much as the queen's dwarf. One day at dinner this malicious little cub was so annoyed with something I had said to him that, raising himself upon the frame of her Majesty's chair, he took me up by the middle and let me drop into a large bowl of cream. Then he ran away as fast as he could.

I fell head over heels, and if I had not been a good swimmer, it might have gone very hard with me, for Glumdalclitch in that instant happened to be at

the other end of the room and the queen was in such a fright, that she lacked the presence of mind to assist me. But my little nurse ran to my relief and took me out after I had swallowed above a quart of cream. I was put to bed. However, I received no other damage than the loss of a suit of clothes. The dwarf was soundly whipped and as a further punishment, forced to drink up the bowl of cream. Soon after, the queen gave him to a lady of quality, so that I saw him no more, to my great satisfaction.

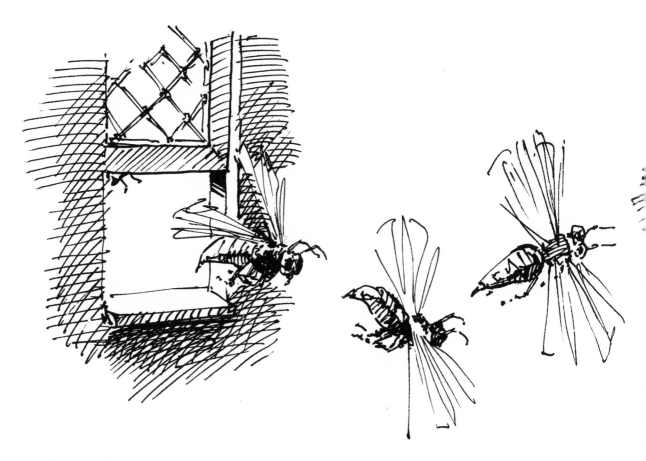

I remember one morning when Glumdalclitch had set me in my box upon a window, as she usually did in fair days to give me air, I lifted up one of my sashes and sat down at my table to eat a piece of sweetcake. Suddenly more than twenty wasps came flying into the room humming louder than the drones of as many bagpipes. Some of them seized pieces of my cake. Others flew about my head, confounding me with the noise and putting me in the utmost terror of their stings.

However I had the courage to rise and draw my sword and attack them in the air. I dispatched four of them, but the rest got away, and I quickly shut my window. These insects were as large as partridges. I took out their stings, found them an inch and a half long and as sharp as needles. I carefully preserved them all and have since shown them with some other curiosities in several parts of Europe.

# CHAPTER FOUR

I should have lived happy enough in that country if my littleness had not exposed me to several troublesome accidents, some of which I shall venture to relate.

Glumdalclitch often carried me into the gardens of the court in my box and would sometimes take me out of it and hold me in her hand or set me down to walk. I remember, before the dwarf left the queen, he followed us one day into those gardens. My nurse having set me down near some dwarf appletrees, I showed my wit by a silly allusion between him and the trees which happens to hold in their language as it does in ours. Afterward, when I was walking under one of them, the malicious rogue shook it directly over my head. A dozen apples, each of them near as large as a barrel, came tumbling about my ears. One of them hit me on the back and knocked me down flat on my face.

A more dangerous accident happened to me in the same garden when my little nurse, believing she had put me in a secure place, and having left my box at home, went to another part of the gardens.

While she was absent and out of hearing, a small white spaniel belonging to one of the chief gardeners, happened to come near the place where I lay. Following the scent, the dog came directly up, and taking me in his mouth, ran straight to his master, wagging his tail, and set me gently on the ground. By good fortune, he had been so well taught that I was carried between his teeth without the least hurt.

The poor gardener, who had a great liking for me, was in a terrible fright. He gently took me up in both his hands and asked me how I was. But I was so out of breath that I could not speak a word. In a few minutes I came to myself and he carried me safe to my little nurse, who by this time had returned to the place where she left me and was in agonies when I did not appear, nor answer when she called. She scolded the gardener on account of his dog. But the thing was hushed up and never known at court, for the girl was afraid of the queen's anger.

This accident determined Glumdalclitch never to trust me out of her sight in the future. I had been long afraid of this resolution and therefore con-

cealed from her some little adventures that happened in those times when I was left by myself.

Once a hawk hovering over the garden made a swoop at me, and if I had not resolutely drawn my sword and run under a thick trellis, he would have certainly carried me away in his talons. Another time, walking to the top of a fresh molehill, I fell to my neck in the hole through which that animal had cast up the earth.

I cannot tell whether I was more pleased or horrified to observe that the smaller birds did not appear to be at all afraid of me. One day I took a thick cudgel and threw it at a linnet with all my strength so luckily that I knocked him down. Seizing him with both my hands, I ran with him in triumph to

my nurse. However, the bird, who had only been stunned, recovered himself and gave me so many boxes with his wings that I was twenty times thinking to let him go. But I was soon relieved by one of our servants, who wrung the bird's neck, and I had him the next day for dinner by the queen's command. This linnet, as near as I can remember, seemed to be somewhat larger than an English swan.

The queen, who often used to hear me talk of my sea voyages, asked me whether I understood how to handle a sail or an oar and whether a little exercise at rowing might not be convenient for my health. I answered that I understood both very well, but I could not see how this could be done in their country, where the smallest rowboat was equal to a first-rate man-of-war among us and such a boat as I could manage would never live in any of their rivers.

Her Majesty said, if I would describe a boat, her own carpenter should make it and she would provide a place for me to sail in. The fellow was an ingenious workman and in ten days finished a pleasure-boat able to hold eight people of my size.

When it was finished, the queen was so delighted that she ran with it to the king, who ordered it to be put in a cistern full of water, with me in it, by way of trial, though I could not manage my little oars for want of room. The queen then ordered the carpenter to make a wooden trough three hundred feet long, fifty broad, and eight deep. This was placed on the floor along the wall, in an outer room of the palace. It had a drain near the bottom to let out the water when it began to grow stale, and two servants could easily fill it in half an hour.

Here I often used to row for my diversion, as well as that of the queen and her ladies. Sometimes I would put up my sail and then my business was only to steer while the ladies gave me a gale with their fans. When they were weary, some of the pages would blow my sail forward with their breath while I showed my art by steering starboard or larboard as I pleased.

Another time one of the servants, whose job it was to fill my trough every third day with fresh water, was so careless as to let a huge frog slip out of his pail. The frog lay concealed until I was put into my boat, but then, seeing a

resting place, climbed up onto the boat and made it lean so much on one side that I was forced to balance it with all my weight on the other to prevent overturning. When the frog had gotten in, it hopped the length of the boat and then over my head, daubing my face and clothes with its slime. The largeness of its features made it appear the most deformed animal that can be conceived. However, I wanted Glumdalclitch to let me deal with it alone. I banged it a good while with one of my oars and at last forced it to leap out of the boat.

But the greatest danger I ever underwent in that kingdom was from a monkey who belonged to one of the servants in the kitchen. Glumdalclitch had locked me in her closet while she went somewhere to visit. The weather being very warm, the closet window was left open, as well as the windows and the door of my box. As I sat quietly at my table, I heard something

bounce in at the closet window and skip about from one side to the other. Then I saw this animal, leaping up and down, until at last he came to my box, which he seemed to view with great curiosity, peeping in at every window.

After some time spent in peeping, grinning and chattering, he at last spied me, and reaching one of his paws in the door, as a cat does when she plays with a mouse, he seized the lapel of my coat and dragged me out. He took me up in his right forefoot, and when I offered to struggle, he squeezed me so hard, that I thought it better to submit.

He was interrupted by a noise at the closet door, as if somebody were opening it, whereupon he suddenly leaped up to the window at which he had come in, and from there upon the gutters, walking upon three legs and holding me in the fourth, until he clambered up to a roof that was next to ours.

I heard Glumdalclitch give a shriek at the moment the monkey was carrying me out. The palace was all in an uproar. The servants ran for ladders. The monkey was seen by hundreds in the court, sitting upon the ridge of a building, holding me like a baby in one of his forepaws and feeding me with the other by cramming into my mouth some food he had squeezed out of one side of his cheeks, and patting me when I would not eat. Many of the rabble below could not help laughing. Neither do I think they ought to be blamed, for, without question, the sight was ridiculous enough to everybody but myself.

The ladders were now applied and mounted by several men. The monkey observed this, and finding himself almost surrounded and not being able to make speed enough with his three legs, he let me drop on a ridge-tile and made his escape. Here I sat for some time, five hundred yards from the ground, expecting every moment to be blown down by the wind. But an honest lad climbed up and putting me into his breeches pocket, brought me down safe.

I was almost choked with the filthy stuff the monkey had crammed down my throat. But my dear little nurse picked it out of my mouth with a small needle. Yet I was so weak and bruised with the squeezes given me by this hateful animal that I was forced to keep to my bed for two weeks. The king, queen, and all the court, asked every day after my health.

# CHAPTER FIVE

I used to attend the king's bath once or twice a week and had often seen him under the barber's hand, which indeed was at first terrible to behold. For the razor was almost twice as long as an ordinary scythe. His Majesty, according to the custom of the country, was only shaved twice a week.

The king, who delighted in music, had frequent concerts at court to which I was sometimes carried. But the noise was so great that I could hardly distinguish the tunes. I am confident that all the drums and trumpets of a royal army, beating and sounding together just at your ears, could not equal it. My practice was to have my box removed as far as I could from the places where the performers sat. Then I would shut the doors and windows and draw the window-curtains, after which I found their music not disagreeable.

I had learned in my youth to play a little upon the spinet. Glumdalclitch kept one in her chamber and a master attended twice a week, to teach her. A fancy came into my head, that I would entertain the king and queen with an

English tune upon this instrument. This appeared extremely difficult, for with my arms extended, I could not reach more than five keys and to press them down required a good stroke with my fist, which would be too great a labor and to no purpose.

The method I contrived was this: I prepared two round sticks about the bigness of common cudgels. They were thicker at one end than the other. I covered the thicker end with a piece of a mouse's skin. A bench was placed before the spinet, slightly below the keys, and I was put upon the bench. I ran sideways upon it that way and this, as fast as I could, banging the proper keys with my two sticks to play a jig to the great satisfaction of both their Majesties. It was the most violent exercise I ever underwent, and yet I could not strike above sixteen keys, nor, consequently, play the bass and treble together as other artists do, which was a great disadvantage to my performance.

The king's library, more than a thousand volumes, is in a gallery of twelve hundred feet long. I had permission to borrow what books I pleased.

The queen's carpenter had made a kind of wooden machine, formed like a standing ladder. It was indeed a movable pair of stairs.

The book I had a mind to read was put up leaning against the wall. I first mounted to the upper step of the ladder, and turning my face toward the book, began at the top of the page, and walked to the right and left about eight or ten paces, according to the length of the lines. As I got a little below the level of my eyes I would descend gradually until I came to the bottom. After which I mounted again and began the other page in the same manner, and so turned over the leaf, which I could easily do with both my hands, for it was as thick and stiff as pasteboard.

# CHAPTER SIX

I had always a strong desire that I should sometime recover my liberty. Although I was indeed treated with much kindness, I could never forget those domestic pledges I had left behind me. I wanted to be among people with whom I could converse upon equal terms, and walk about the streets and fields without fear of being trod to death like a frog or young puppy.

I had now been two years in this country, and about the beginning of the third, Glumdalclitch and I joined the king and the queen in a journey to the south coast of the kingdom.

I was carried as usual in my traveling box, which, as I have described, was a closet twelve feet wide. I had ordered a hammock to be fixed by silken ropes from the four corners at the top to break the jolts when a servant carried me before him on horseback. On the roof of my closet, set not directly over the middle of the hammock, I ordered the carpenter to cut out a hole of a foot square to give me air in hot weather as I slept.

When we came to our journey's end, the king decided to pass a few days at a palace he had near Flanflasnic, a city within eighteen English miles of the seaside. Glumdalclitch and I were much fatigued—I had caught a small cold but the poor girl was so ill as to be confined to her chamber.

I longed to see the ocean, which must be the scene of my escape, if ever it should happen. I pretended to be worse than I really was and desired leave to take the fresh air of the sea with a page whom I was very fond of and who had sometimes been trusted with me. I shall never forget with what unwillingness Glumdalclitch consented, bursting at the same time into a flood of tears, as if she had some foreboding of what was to happen.

The boy took me out in my box about half an hour's walk from the palace, toward the rocks on the seashore. I ordered him to set me down, and lifting up one of my windows, I cast many a wistful melancholy look toward the sea. I found myself not feeling well and told the page that I had a mind to take a nap in my hammock. I got in and the boy shut the window to keep out the cold.

I soon fell asleep, and suddenly I found myself awakened with a violent pull upon the ring which was fastened at the top of my box for the conve-

nience of carriage. I felt the box raised very high in the air, and then born forward with enormous speed. The first jolt almost shook me out of my hammock, but afterwards the motion was easy enough. I called out several times as loud as I could raise my voice, but all to no purpose. I looked toward my windows and could see nothing but the clouds and sky.

I heard a noise just over my head like the clapping of wings and then began to understand the woeful condition I was in: Some eagle had gotten the ring of my box in his beak, with an intent to let it fall on a rock like a tortoise in a shell and then pick out my body and devour it.

In a little time I observed the flutter of wings to increase very fast, and my box was tossed up and down like a signboard on a windy day. All of a sudden I felt myself falling for more than a minute, but with such incredible swiftness that I almost lost my breath. My fall was stopped by a terrible splash that sounded louder to my ears than the falls of Niagara. After this I was quite in the dark for another minute, and then my box began to rise so high that I could see light from the tops of my windows. I now saw that I had fallen into the sea.

I suppose that the eagle which had flown away with my box was pursued

by two or three others and forced to let me drop while he was defending himself against the rest, who hoped to share in the prey. The plates of iron fastened to the bottom of the box preserved the balance and prevented it from being broken on the surface of the water.

How often did I then wish myself with my dear Glumdalclitch, from whom one single hour had so far divided me! I expected every moment to see my box dashed in pieces or at least upset by a rising wave. In this disconsolate state, I heard, or at least thought I heard, some kind of grating noise on that side of my box where the staples were fixed.

This gave me some faint hopes of relief. I ventured to unscrew one of my chairs, which were always fastened to the floor, and screwing it down again directly under the slip-board that I had lately opened, I mounted on the chair, and putting my mouth as near as I could to the hole, I called for help in a loud voice and in all the languages I understood. I then fastened my handkerchief to a stick I usually carried, and thrusting it up the hole, waved it several times in the air so that if any boat were near, the seamen might conjecture some unhappy mortal to be shut up in the box.

In return, I heard a great shout repeated three times, giving me transports of joy.

I now heard a trampling over my head and somebody calling through the hole with a loud voice in the English tongue: "If there be anybody below, let him speak."

I answered, I was an Englishman, drawn by ill fortune into the greatest calamity that ever any creature underwent, and begged to be delivered out of the dungeon I was in.

The voice replied, my box was fastened to their ship, and the carpenter would come and saw a hole in the cover large enough to pull me out.

I answered that there was no need to do more than tell one of the crew to put his finger into the ring and take the box out of the sea into the ship. Some of them upon hearing me talk so wildly thought I was mad. Others laughed, for indeed it never came into my head that I was now among people of my own stature and strength. The carpenter came and in a few minutes sawed a passage about four feet square. Then he let down a small ladder, upon which I mounted, and from there I was taken into the ship in a very weak condition.

The sailors were all in amazement and asked me a thousand questions which I had no inclination to answer. I was equally confounded at the sight of so many pygmies, for such I took them to be after having so long accustomed my eyes to the monstrous objects I had left.

The captain, Mr. Thomas Wilcocks, observing I was ready to faint, took me into his cabin, gave me a cordial to comfort me, and advised me to take a little rest, of which I had great need.

I slept some hours and upon waking I found myself much recovered. It was now about eight o'clock at night, and the captain ordered supper immediately.

He entertained me with great kindness, seeing that I did not look mad. He said that about twelve o'clock at noon, as he was looking through his glass, he spied it at a distance and thought it was a sail. Upon coming nearer, he sent out his long-boat to discover what I was. His men had come back in a fright, swearing they had seen a swimming house. But he laughed at their folly and went himself in the boat, ordering his men to take a strong cable along with them. The weather being calm, he had rowed around me several times. He also discovered the two staples upon the one side which was all of boards. He had then commanded his men to row up to that side, and fastening a cable to one of the staples, he had ordered his men to tow my chest towards the ship. When it was there, he gave directions to fasten another cable to the ring fixed in the cover and to raise up my chest with pulleys. He said they saw my stick and handkerchief thrust out of the hole and concluded that some unhappy man must be shut up in the cabinet.

I begged the captain to hear me tell my story, which I faithfully did, from the last time I left England to the moment he first discovered me. And, as truth always forces its way into rational minds, so this worthy gentleman, who had very good sense, was immediately convinced of my candor.

Further to confirm all I had said, I asked him to give order that my cabinet should be brought. I opened it in his presence and showed him the small collection of rarities. There was the comb I had made out of the stumps of the king's beard, and another of the same materials, but fixed into a paring of her Majesty's thumbnail, which served for the back.

There was a collection of needles and pins from a foot to half a yard long, four wasp-stings, some combings of the queen's hair and a gold ring which one day she made me a present of, taking it from her little finger and throwing it over my head like a collar. I asked the captain to please accept this ring in return for his politeness, which he absolutely refused.

I could force nothing on him but a tooth. I had observed him to examine it with great curiosity and found he had a fancy for it. He received it with abundance of thanks. It was pulled by a surgeon from one of Glumdalclitch's men who was afflicted with the toothache. It was about a foot long, and four inches in diameter.

The captain wondered at one thing very much, which was to hear me speak so loud, and he asked me whether the king or queen of that country were hard of hearing. I told him it was what I had been used to for more than two years, and that I admired as much the voices of him and his men, who seemed to me only to whisper, and yet I could hear them well enough. But when I spoke in that country, it was like a man talking in the street, to another looking out from the top of a steeple, unless I was placed upon a table or held in any person's hand.

The captain called in at one or two ports, but I never went out of the ship until we came to England, which was on the 3rd day of June, 1706, about nine months after my escape.

When I came to my own house, my wife ran out to embrace me, but I stooped lower than her knees, thinking she could otherwise never be able to reach my mouth. My daughter kneeled to ask my blessing, but I could not see her until she arose, having been so long used to standing with my head and eyes raised to over sixty feet. And then I went to take her up with one hand, by the waist. I looked down upon the servants as if they had been pygmies and I a giant. In short, I behaved myself so mysteriously that they were all of the captain's opinion, when he first saw me and concluded I had lost my wits.

In a little time, I and my family and friends came to a right understanding, but my wife insisted I should never go to sea any more.